JEREMY STRONG once worked in a bakery, putting the jam into three thousand doughnuts every night. Now he puts the jam in stories instead, which he finds much more exciting. At the age of three, he fell out of a first-floor bedroom window and landed on his head. His mother says that this damaged him for the rest of his life and refuses to take any responsibility. He loves writing stories because he says it is 'the only time you alone have complete control and can make anything happen'. His ambition is to make you laugh (or at least snuffle). Jeremy Strong lives near Bath with his wife, Gillie, four cats and a flying cow.

ARE YOU FEELING SILLY ENOUGH TO READ MORE?

THE BATTLE FOR CHRISTMAS (A COSMIC PYJAMAS ADVENTURE)

THE BEAK SPEAKS

BEWARE! KILLER TOMATOES

CARTOON KID

CHICKEN SCHOOL

CHRISTMAS CHAOS FOR THE HUNDRED-MILE-AN-HOUR DOG

DINOSAUR POX

DOCTOR BONKERS! (A COSMIC PYJAMAS ADVENTURE)

GIANT JIM AND THE HURRICANE

THE HUNDRED-MILE-AN-HOUR DOG

KRANKENSTEIN'S CRAZY HOUSE OF HORROR
(A COSMIC PYJAMAS ADVENTURE)

KRAZY COW SAVES THE WORLD – WELL, ALMOST

LOST! THE HUNDRED-MILE-AN-HOUR DOG

MY BROTHER'S FAMOUS BOTTOM

MY BROTHER'S HOT CROSS BOTTOM

THERE'S A PHARAOH IN OUR BATH!

JEREMY STRONG'S LAUGH-YOUR-SOCKS-OFF JOKE BOOK
JEREMY STRONG'S LAUGH-YOUR-SOCKS-OFF EVEN MORE JOKE BOOK
JEREMY STRONG'S LAUGH-YOUR-SOCKS-OFF CLASSROOM CHAOS JOKE BOOK

LAUGH YOUR SOCKS OFF WITH

JEREMY STRONG

CARTOON KID SUPERCHARGED!

ILLUSTRATED BY
STEVE MAY

PUFFIN

PUFFIN BOOKS

Published by the Penguin Group
Penguin Books Ltd, 80 Strand, London WC2R 0RL, England
Penguin Group (USA) Inc., 375 Hudson Street, New York, New York 10014, USA
Penguin Group (Canada), 90 Eglinton Avenue East, Suite 700, Toronto, Ontario, Canada M4P 2Y3
(a division of Pearson Penguin Canada Inc.)
Penguin Ireland, 25 St Stephen's Green, Dublin 2, Ireland (a division of Penguin Books Ltd)
Penguin Group (Australia), 250 Camberwell Road, Camberwell, Victoria 3124, Australia
(a division of Pearson Australia Group Pty Ltd)
Penguin Books India Pvt Ltd, 11 Community Centre, Panchsheel Park, New Delhi – 110 017, India
Penguin Group (NZ), 67 Apollo Drive, Rosedale, North Shore 0632, New Zealand
(a division of Pearson New Zealand Ltd)
Penguin Books (South Africa) (Pty) Ltd, 24 Sturdee Avenue, Rosebank, Johannesburg 2196, South Africa

Penguin Books Ltd, Registered Offices: 80 Strand, London WC2R 0RL, England

puffinbooks.com

First published 2011
001 – 10 9 8 7 6 5 4 3 2 1

Text copyright © Jeremy Strong, 2011
Illustrations copyright © Steve May, 2011
All rights reserved

Except in the Unite   ion that it shall not,
by way of trade or oth   without the publisher's
prior consent in any   plished and without
a similar condi   ent purchaser

A CIP   Library

ISBN: 978–0–141–33475–2

www.greenpenguin.co.uk

MIX
Paper from
responsible sources
FSC
www.fsc.org   FSC™ C018179

Penguin Books is committed to a sustainable
future for our business, our readers and our
planet. This book is made from paper certified
by the Forest Stewardship Council.

*For my mother, with love
and thanks for everything.
Well, almost everything, but not
he stewed oxtail, the liver or the
spit-wet face-cleaning service.*

CONTENTS

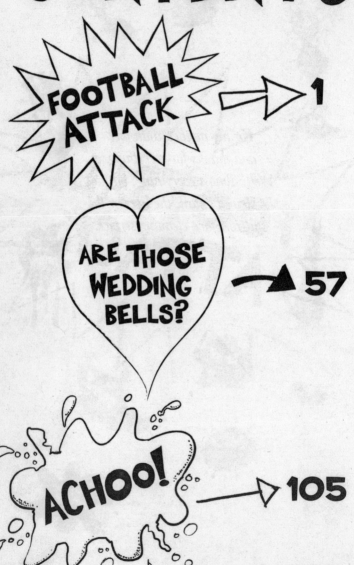

TSSSSSSS!
GRRRRRR!

That's the noise Masher McNee makes when
he's angry. It probably means he's plotting
something terrible, like How To Destroy
The School, or quite possibly the WHOLE
PLANET.

Masher McNee spells BIG TROUBLE, I can tell you. (Well, OBVIOUSLY, '*Masher McNee*' spells 'Masher McNee' and '*big trouble*' spells 'big trouble', but you know what I mean. You're NOT MR STUPIDO, like Masher, are you?!)

And why was Masher so cross? I will tell you.
Because my class had just won THE ETHEL
SNUFFLEBOTTOM COMPETITION
FOR THE BEST CLASS IN THE WHOLE
SCHOOL.

That was some competition! Masher McNee

and his Monster Mob tried to cheat really,
REALLY hard, but we got the better of them,
even though they are BIGGER and OLDER
than us.

We won because we are SUPERHEROES!
Mr Butternut, our teacher, told us that.

As for me, I'm Casper the Cartoon Kid. I'm called that because I'm always doodling and drawing, as you can see. Then there's Pete, my best friend, also known as Big Feet Pete (for obvious reasons!).

Now Masher McNee is out for REVENGE.
He's not a superhero – just a big bully.
Basically he wants to mash Pete and me into
little bits. Not to mention my classmates,
like Cameron and Mia. (Mia is Pete's
GIRLFRIEND and she's got more curls than
a poodle in a Best Curly Poodle Competition.
That's why we call her Curly-Wurly-Girly.)

WOOF!

BEST
POODLE

We are all in Mr Butternut's class and it's the best class to be in because he's brilliant (except when he's being Mr Horrible Hairy Face, which he is sometimes because he's a teacher and that's what they do. You know what they're like.)

I don't know what Masher is planning so it makes me a bit twitchy. But hey, LIFE GOES ON! That's what Mr Butternut says when we get upset.

PUT IT BEHIND YOU. LIFE GOES ON.

It's all very well for Mr Butternut to say that – he's big and his beard makes him look TOUGH, like a Viking. Anyhow, it's fine for

Mr Butternut to say *'Put it behind you'*, but I certainly wouldn't like to put Masher McNee behind me! I would need eyes in the back of my head.

Masher has been cruising the playground, making threatening noises every time he passes us.

Anyhow, we got to the end of the school day and Masher hadn't turned us into ketchup, so that was OK. As we left the classroom Mr Butternut stood at the door and gave us all some homework.

'Tomorrow I would like you to bring something old to school. Something old that you treasure.'

Pete and I looked at Mr Butternut as if he was mad. Well, he probably is, but in a nice way. Teachers are sometimes, aren't they? Mad.

'Something old and treasured?' I repeated.
'I don't keep *old* things. I throw them away
because they're – because they're – OLD!'

'Me too,' Pete agreed gloomily.

Sarah Sitterbout didn't have a problem
with the homework at all. But then Sarah
Sitterbout's brain is as big as a whole
LIBRARY of encyclopaedias.

She knows EVERYTHING – except what colour my pants are – ha ha!

'They're blue, Casper,' Sarah announced flatly. 'I'm going to bring my fluffy toy rabbit, Cuggles. He's as old as me, just about.'

And she went walking off, wearing a big grin.

I was gobsmacked!

'How did she know that?' I asked Pete.

'Because she has X-ray eyes, my little ginger twiglet pal! Uh-oh, watch out,' he warned. 'Snotbox alert.'

Hartley Tartly-Green went strutting past with his nose in the air. 'I'm going to show everyone my new model train. It's a steam train called *The Mallard*. It used to hold the record for the fastest train in the world. My grandfather rode on it once.'

Pete snorted loudly. 'Your grandfather must be incredibly small if he rode on a toy train. How did he open the door and get in?'

Hartley stopped and stared at Pete.

'Well, my steam train is brand new and it's better than anything you'll bring. *So there* back to you and *murrgh-murrgh-murrgh* on top. Twice.' No wonder we call him Snotbox.

SARAH SITTERBOUT'S BIT ABOUT STEAM TRAINS

Steam trains were used for many years before diesel and electric trains took over. One of the fastest steam trains ever was *The Mallard*. In 1938 it reached a speed of over 125 miles an hour, making it the fastest train in the world. Mallards are actually a kind of duck. When mallards quack it sounds as if they are laughing. I have no idea why anyone would give a steam train the name of a DUCK - especially a laughing one. I think that's daft.

QUACK!

By the time we reached home Pete and I still hadn't thought of anything old or treasured to take into school. I went up to my bedroom and hunted around. I was hoping to find something amazing, but all I could see was Colin, my pet chameleon.

What? But surely I'm a real treasure?

I did wonder about taking him into school, but he's only two. That means he's not even ready for nursery yet, and he's not exactly a treasure, either.

Then Pete came round. He said he was looking for his hamster, Betty. She's always trying to escape, but I certainly hadn't seen her. Then he started going on about how boring his mum's boyfriend is. He's called Derek, but Pete calls him Uncle Boring because that's what he is – boring. Anyway, talking about Uncle Boring gave me an idea and it was a pretty good one.

'Pete! I know what to do. I shall take my great-gran into school tomorrow!'

'What?! Gee-Gee? The one in the Care Home?'

'Exactly.' I answered.

Gee-Gee is my dad's granny, so that makes her my great-gran. She is amazing. For a start, she is EIGHTY-NINE, and that's REALLY old – it's almost prehistoric. I mean, Gee-Gee probably fought dinosaurs and stuff.

GRRR!

If you think she's got a funny name, that's her fault. She *told* us to call her that.

IT'S DOUBLE G, GEE-GEE, FOR GREAT-GRAN. AND BECAUSE AFTER I DIE I WANT TO COME BACK AS A HORSE.

Gee-Gee is amazing. She used to live in Darkest Africa when she was a child. She's always telling me eye-boggling stories about lions jumping on her tent at night and things like that.

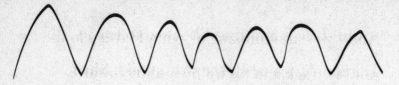

I told Mum my plan. 'Gee-Gee is old *and* she's treasured. I'm going to take her into school tomorrow morning.'

Do you know what my mum did? She burst out laughing. 'I don't think Mr Butternut meant you to bring in your great-gran,' she chuckled. 'He meant something like a photograph album or an old toy. That sort of thing. Silly boy!'

Huh. You can imagine what I was thinking when she suggested an old toy. I was thinking of Hartley Tartly-Green and his steam train.

And I was also thinking of tying Hartley to the railway track and his train chuffing towards him.

'Anyhow,' Mum shrugged. 'You can't take Great-Gran into school tomorrow because the doctor is coming to see her.'

My spirits sank all the way down to my ankles.

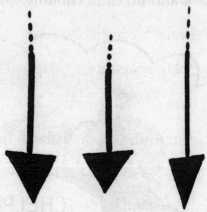

'She's seeing the doctor? What's wrong with her?

'She's eighty-nine,' Mum explained.

What kind of answer was THAT? Since when has eighty-nine been an illness? I stomped back upstairs and gave Pete the news. We sat on my bed in silence with our knees hunched up to our chests.

Pete suddenly sat up straight. 'Bouncing bananas!' he cried. 'Your great-gran keeps a wheelchair here, doesn't she?' He grinned and slapped me on the back. 'Do not worry, knobbly-kneed mini-person. All will be well.' He leaned closer and whispered his plan into my left ear.

UH-OH!
Pete has an idea . . .

I MIGHT HAVE KNOBBLY KNEES, BUT YOUR FEET ARE THE SIZE OF NUCLEAR SUBMARINES.

The next morning I set off for school as usual. Although it wasn't quite as usual because first of all I nipped round the back of the house, nicked Great-Gran's spare wheelchair and whizzed it up the road.

As I passed Pete's house he came hurrying out, his school bag bulging. 'I've got everything!' Pete cried triumphantly.

I clapped him on the back..'Fantastic! We are Team Numero Uno!'

We hid round the corner while Pete got changed. Yep – you've got it! Pete was going to be my great-gran! He'd pinched an old, old dress of his mum's, a walking stick and dark glasses. The final touch was a baseball cap pulled down low to hide his face.

I'm not sure the baseball cap looked right, but it was the best way to hide the fact that Pete is nine, not eighty-nine.

Our class was already filing into the classroom. There was Sarah Sitterbout with Cuggles. There was Hartley Tartly-Green with his snazzy train. There was Mia with a photo of her mum as a little girl in Italy. There was Cameron with a ginormous pumpkin. What?!

I like Cameron. We call him the BFC, or Big
Friendly Cameron, because he is SO tall and
friendly. He's even friendly with trees and likes
hugging them.

1
256
356
512

Mr Butternut was mightily surprised when I pushed Great-Gran up to the door. 'Who's this?' he asked.

'My great-gran. She's eighty-nine,' I declared hopefully. 'Which makes her VERY old – AND she's a treasure.'

Pete waved a hand, but didn't look up. 'You may call me madam,' he said in a low, shaky voice. He was trying to be like Gee-Gee, but sounded more like a frog stuck in a spin dryer.

Mr Butternut gave a little bow. He did! 'I'm
very pleased to meet you, madam,' he said.
And he took Pete's hand and kissed it! HE
DID! HE KISSED PETE'S HAND! I nearly
died.

BLUUUUURGH!!!

Pete snatched his hand away and wiped it
on his dress. 'Stop slobbering all over me,'
he began in his own voice and then quickly

changed to the frog in a spin dryer. 'I'm a married woman. At least I was until my husband died.'

'I'm sorry to hear that,' said Mr Butternut.

'So you should be, young man. A pie killed him. He was only forty-two.' Pete gave a loud sniff and dabbed at his nose with one sleeve.

Mr Butternut frowned. 'It must have been a very large pie.'

'Not at all.' Pete charged on, getting himself into an even deeper mess. 'It wasn't large, but it was very heavy. There was a horseshoe in it.'

Mr Butternut clapped a hand to his forehead.

'The pie had a horseshoe in it? How did that get there?'

ARE YOU THE POLICE? STOP ASKING QUESTIONS!

I hurriedly pushed Great-Granny Pete forward. 'Excuse me, Mr Butternut, I think Great-Gran's a bit tired.'

Mr Butternut moved aside and I wheeled Pete into class, bending forward over his shoulder.

'What do you think you're doing, fuzz-brain? Pies with horseshoes in them?'

'It's not my fault. She's your great-granny! What am I supposed to say?' Pete complained. 'Old people always talk rubbish like that, don't they?'

'No, they don't, Pete. Just keep your mouth shut and behave yourself. Pretend you're asleep or something.'

34

Pete managed to keep quiet after that, even when Hartley Fartly wandered past and muttered that my great-gran was weird. A claw flashed out from the wheelchair and seized Hartley's wrist.

I have all of my own teeth. Why would I want anyone else's?

'I heard that, you horrible, weedy weasel. How dare you! I'm eighty-nine and I still have all my own teeth.'

'Sorry! Sorry! So sorry!' squeaked Hartley, absolutely terrified. He raced back to his seat and sat down. He didn't stop trembling for ten minutes.

Pete's shoulders heaved with laughter.

Breaktime came and we went out to the playground. I parked Great-Gran Pete at one side. AND THAT was when Masher McNee came strolling up with his Mob.

'I heard you've got your great-gran with you today,' sneered Masher. 'Still need someone to

WHAT'S MASHER UP TO?

look after you, babyface?'

'Go and get lost,' I said, rather bravely, I thought. I reckoned Masher wouldn't do anything while I had Great-Gran nearby.

Masher just laughed. 'Thought you and your friends might like a game of footer with me and my friends,' he suggested innocently. 'You know, friendly, like.'

I WONDER WHY PETE ISN'T AT SCHOOL TODAY?

'Sounds good to me,' said Cameron, who thinks everyone should be friends, especially with trees.

'I'm up for it,' declared Mia. She's a football fanatic.

'That's good,' smirked Masher. 'Meet the rest of my team.' Do you know who it was? Only Gory and Tory, THE VAMPIRE TWINS!

'We're on!' shouted Masher. 'Let's go! Our goal is over there,' he added, pointing to the far end of the playground. 'Yours is HERE,' he announced, dropping the ball and kicking it straight in. 'GOAL!' he yelled. 'One–nil to us!'

I was boiling with anger. I grabbed the ball and took kick-off, but Masher tripped me even before my foot touched it. He dribbled straight up to our end where the goal was wide open.

It was a disaster in the making.

And then Great-Gran leaped out of her wheelchair and got on the ball. Masher's

team were so astonished they just stood and watched. Pete had a clear run, slammed the ball into their goal, wandered back to the wheelchair and sat down.

I picked myself out of the dust and grinned at Masher. 'One-all, I think.'

'Hey!' yelled Masher. 'Your granny can't be on your team!'

'Why not?' I countered. 'You've got Gory and Tory.'

Masher was lost for words. He took the ball and went for kick-off. After that things began to get really dirty. Masher's team were fouling all the time, kicking our legs from under us and all sorts.

This was how he was getting his revenge over the best class trophy. This was his way of mashing us into little bits.

However, they didn't dare attack Great-Gran because they thought she was an old lady. Ha ha ha! Pete scored two more goals, from the wheelchair! He's pretty good at footer, which is hardly surprising considering the size of his feet.

AND THEN –

AAARRRGH!

MUCHO PROBLEMO!!

'Casper! I've brought Gee-Gee for you!' Mum called to me.

'The doctor cancelled his visit.'

She suddenly noticed the other Great-
Gran whizzing up and down and playing
football.

'What's going on?' Mum demanded. 'Who's
that old lady with the baseball cap?'

IT LOOKS
AS IF I HAVE
COMPETITION.

'Is that your great-gran?' asked Masher, looking across to Gee-Gee and then back towards Pete, still cruising the playground.

I could almost see Masher's brain working. (He does have one, I think, but it's about the size of a baked bean's baby bean.) Things were slowly beginning to make sense and then –

POP!

It came into his head.

'So if THAT is your great-gran, WHO is scoring all those GOALS?!' Masher's eyes burned holes in Pete's back. 'And where is your great pal Pete, eh? Eh? EH?'

But Gee-Gee wasn't going to have any of that.

'That looks like a bit of a ding-dong,' she muttered. A moment later she spun her wheels so fast they spat gravel all over Mum's feet.

'I'm not putting up with any of this nonsense,' shouted Gee-Gee, as I raced after her, trying to keep up. 'I'm not scared of a bunch of gangsters. I wrestled tigers in Africa.'

'Gee-Gee, there aren't any tigers in Africa,' I panted.

'That's because they were so scared of me they ran away,' she yelled back.

48

By this time it looked as if Masher and his pals were about to murder anyone they could lay their hands on. There was only one thing for it. It was superhero time!

But it didn't happen *quite* like that. Masher McNee was not the only one who had rumbled us.

Mr Butternut had turned into Mr Horrible Hairy Face and my mum was doing her nut.

'You've got some explaining to do, young man,' they chorused.

Before I could open my mouth Gee-Gee was spinning the wheels of her chair and she was off again, whizzing across the playground. At first I thought she was after Pete, but all she wanted was the football! Gee-Gee was on it in a flash and she rammed it into Masher's goal.

'You can't do that!' Masher cried.

'Going to stop me, doughnut?' Gee-Gee yelled back. And that's how the football match started up again. By the time the bell went for the end of play, we had lost count of the number of goals Gee-Gee had scored.

'I think we won,' said Gee-Gee with great satisfaction, as I pushed her back to Mum.

Mum watched all this with a sour face. 'Just look at Casper's great grandmother – racing round, doing wheelies, scoring goals, yelling her head off – what kind of example is that?' she grumbled to Mr Butternut. 'And those children are in big trouble too.'

Mr Butternut didn't seem so sure. 'The children? Oh, you can't blame them.'

'What?' cried Mum. 'Why ever not?'

My teacher tugged his beard thoughtfully. 'I was the one who asked them to bring in something old and treasured, so if anyone is

54

to blame it's probably me. As for your grandmother, what a splendid old lady. I hope I'm as perky as that when I'm in a wheelchair.'

I'm telling you, that Mr Butternut is the best teacher EVER!

Mind you, I was still in BIG TROUBLE when I got home. And so were Pete and Gee-Gee. (But it was worth it!)

I don't understand football. Why chase something you can't eat?

GRRRRRR-
GRRRUNTLE-GROAN-SNORTLE-SQUORTLE-MOANY-MOANY.

That's the noise Pete makes when he has spent far too much time with Uncle Boring.

ALWAYS CHEW YOUR FOOD THIRTY-SIX TIMES – BURBLE BURBLE.

BORED

GRRRR, I'VE GOT A POOR SORE KNEE.

He starts snorting like an animal in pain – quite possibly a giraffe with a sore knee – something like that.

'He's driving me bonkers,' moaned Pete. 'He's been droning on all morning about chewing my food thirty-six times.'

I looked at my friend with sympathy. 'Why does it have to be thirty-six?'

'Uncle Boring says it's good for you. It's all because it took me about five seconds to eat my cereal this morning. The next thing is he's going on at me as if I've just committed some major crime, like putting jellyfish in his bath.'

'Have you ever put jellyfish in his bath?' I asked.

Pete threw me a dark glance. 'Not yet.'

'Anyway,' I said, 'how can you possibly chew cereal thirty-six times? It goes all soggy.'

'Exactly. He is Mr Stupido. I've no idea why my mum goes out with him. He's not even good-looking. Mr Horrible Hairy Face is better-looking than Uncle Boring.'

MR BORING

MR BUTTERNUT

And just at that very moment I had a BUTTERLY BRILLIANT idea. I grabbed Pete's arm.

'Why don't you get your mum to go out with Mr Butternut?'

Pete was so stunned he couldn't speak. At last he croaked, 'ARE YOU OUT OF YOUR MIND? HE'S OUR TEACHER! HE'D BE LIKE MY STEPDAD. I'D PROBABLY HAVE TO CALL HIM UNCLE BUTTERNUT!'

'It was just a thought,' I muttered.

Pete put both hands on my shoulders and looked me straight in the eyes. 'Please don't think.'

'Casper, you need a brain to think, and yours is obviously on a very long holiday far, far away from your head. It's probably on Saturn or Jupiter.'

Huh. Sometimes even your bestest-ever friends can be a disappointment to you. I knew for sure that I was on to something. I could help Pete. It was a great idea. Definitely.

So after Pete had gone I went to my room and scrabbled around among my bits and pieces. Finally I found a picture of Pete's mum. It was really a photo of Pete, but his mum just happened to be in it. I cut Pete out of the photo. Then I settled at my desk and wrote a letter. I did it really, REALLY carefully with my bestest-ever grown-up handwriting.

Deer Mr Butternut,

Pleese come to my house for tea on Friday at 5 o'clock.

I hope you like my pickcher.

Mrs Jawolski (Pete's mum)

PS I am a widow.

This is not a good idea!

Actually Pete's mum is not a widow at all, she's divorced, but I thought Mr Butternut would feel sorry for her if he thought her husband was dead. (See? I am THAT clever!)

Mr B would probably comfort her and they would definitely fall in love. Then they'd get married!

And Uncle Boring would disappear forever and ever. Hooray! (And then maybe Pete would come and tell me it was a brilliant idea of mine after all.)

I took the letter into school the next day and slipped it on to Butternut's desk when he wasn't looking.

I put that last bit so he would know it was important. A few minutes later I saw him spot the envelope. Mr Horrible Hairy Face picked it up, frowned, glanced around the class, opened it and read the letter. I watched as his eyebrows slowly slid up his head. He blinked at the letter several times and then scanned the class again. I quickly pretended to be doing my work, but I could feel Mr Butternut was looking at Pete, right next to me. It felt like his eyes were on telescopic stalks.

Mr Butternut didn't say a word. He tucked the letter inside his jacket and then got on with marking our work. Phew – I'd done it! All I had to do now was sit back and wait until five o'clock on Friday.

9 X 6
= AAAARGH!

AND THEN, out of the blue, a massive rhino-sized thought came thundering into my brain.

Somehow I would have to find a way of getting Pete's mum to make a special tea for Friday.

I had two days to work something out. Maybe I could get Pete to invite

ME to tea. Then I could just let Mr Butternut turn up and I would creep away and let them fall in love and

DING DONG BELL

– there's going to be a wedding!

'What are you doing on Friday?' I asked Pete.

'Friday? I haven't got a clue. That's weeks away.'

'It's the day after tomorrow,' said Sarah

Sitterbout, who knows EVERYTHING. She wasn't supposed to be listening (but she was).

Pete shrugged. 'I don't know what I'll be doing on Friday. Probably shouting "Hooray, it's the weekend, we don't have to go to school!", or something like that. Why are you asking, knobbly-kneed twiglet person?'

'No reason, really,' I said. 'It's just that I think we might run out of food on Friday.'

This was supposed to be a

'Your mum could go to the shops,' Pete answered. Obviously the hint wasn't nearly big enough.

'She's got a sore foot,' I invented.

'You could give her a piggy-back.' Pete snorted at his own joke.

Huh. That friend of mine was pretty slow at getting the message. I struggled on.

'Ha ha. Suppose we have nothing left to eat by Friday afternoon? We'll be starving by five o'clock.' This had to work. This hint was as big as the *Titanic*.

SARAH SITTERBOUT'S BIT ABOUT THE *TITANIC*

The *Titanic* was launched in 1912 and was the biggest ship in the world.

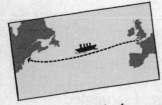

It carried 2,228 passengers and crew. It was supposed to sail between Britain and America, but on its VERY FIRST voyage it hit an iceberg and sank. Was that a mistake, or what? How did that happen? How can you not see a humungously ginormous iceberg in front of

your nose - or in this case, the ship's nose (or *prow*, as it is known to sailors)? 1,523 people drowned, which was a tragedy of iceberg proportions — literally.

'Your dad can do the shopping,' Sarah piped up very matter-of-factly. Thanks a lot, Sarah. That sank the *Titanic* good and proper, didn't it? I watched it vanish beneath the waves.

GLUG GLUG GLUG.

So that was the end of that very-useful-I-don't-think conversation. The day passed without a single idea coming into my head. That evening I lay in bed, trying to think up some clever plan. I tossed and turned all night. My bedclothes ended up in such a twisted

mess, it felt as if I was being spifflicated by a
python.

WHO PUT A
SNAKE IN MY
BED?

Thursday wasn't much better. The only
useful thing about school was that I kept
looking at Mr Butternut and thinking what a
good husband he would make for Pete's mum.
He was kind and good-looking in a crumbly,
teacherish kind of way.

Pete's mum was quite pretty, I suppose. I
mean, she wasn't an ancient hag with a warty
nose or anything like that, but she was getting

on a bit – thirty-
five at least.

The main thing
was that I knew
in my deepest,
deepest self that
I was doing THE
RIGHT THING!
It was going to
work and Uncle
Boring would

soon be nothing more than a distant (horrible)
memory.

I went home with Pete as usual and followed
him into his house. I was hoping something
useful might happen. It started off all right.

'Mrs Jenkinson's got a sore foot,' Pete told his mum.

'Really? Is it bad?' she asked. I seized my chance.

'She can't go shopping,' I said. (Hint hint).

'Maybe *you* can get her shopping, Casper?' Pete's mum said brightly.

AAARRRGH!

Why couldn't anyone just invite me round for tea! It was SO simple and OBVIOUS!

'Or, how about you come to tea at our house tomorrow? I've got chocolate cake that needs using up and I've plenty of food here.'

HOORAY! AT LAST!! I let out a huge sigh

and beamed my uttermost thanks at Pete's
mum.

'Good,' she smiled back. 'Bring your parents
and Abbie. They'll be hungry too.'

NO! NO!! NO!!!

DOUBLE AAARRRGH!

That wasn't supposed to happen. I didn't
want *them* around. They'd get in the way and
muddle things. It was important that Mr
Butternut only had eyes for Pete's mum. Now
I would have to find a way to keep the rest
of my family at home. Huh. If it wasn't one
problem, it was another – in fact it was three
others.

I went back to my house and told my family we'd been invited to tea next door.

Then Abbie and I had a nice argument where she told me she was going out on Friday afternoon anyway. And I said yes, she was probably going to see her BOYFRIEND to have a SNOG.

So then she tried to kill me. I didn't mind. I just tried to kill her back. It's what happens most days.

Anyhow, as things turned out, Dad couldn't come either because he was going to be working overtime. That just left Mum to deal with. And Uncle Boring.

As we left school on Friday, Mr Butternut called after us and winked at Pete.

I'm so glad I'm a chameleon.

Pete was pretty puzzled. 'We won't see him later. And why did he wink at us? I think Mr Horrible Hairy Face is losing his grip on life.

Teachers do, you know. As they get older, they get nuttier.'

We went straight to Pete's house. I was hoping that if I left Mum alone, she would forget the time and not come round for tea. Pete's mum was busy getting the table ready, while Uncle Boring watched.

I don't know how Pete puts up with Derek. He really is the most boring man in the whole wide world. All he does is wander around telling people how to do things.

'You mustn't carry your bag like that, Peter. It will make you lopsided. You should always carry a bag on your back or clutched to your front.'

So Mr Clever Clogs Pete said: 'Why does my bag have a handle if you're not supposed to carry it?'

'That's because the bag makers don't know any better,' answered Uncle Boring evenly. 'Now, if I was a bag maker I would make sure you put them on your back or your front.'

I suddenly thought of a way to get rid of Derek.

'That's very interesting,' I told him. 'I bet you could find out lots more interesting things about bags in the library down the road. Why don't you go and see?'

Uncle Boring said he loved libraries, but he only ever went to the library if it was Tuesday.

I had to think of something to get rid of him. 'Did you know you've got a flat tyre on your car?' I asked.

Uncle Boring stood quite still and stared at me for several seconds. At last he spoke.

'That is very strange.'

'Really?' I croaked. 'Why?

'Because I don't have a car.' said Uncle Boring.

I might have known!

Then he started droning on about using buses and how there was one bus he liked best. 'It's the number fifty-seven. It's yellow and I call her Doris.'

'There's a bus you call Doris?' repeated Pete in disbelief.

Uncle Boring nodded and smiled. Pete and I looked at each other. Sometimes the world of adults seemed very, VERY strange.

By now I was panicking. Mr Butternut would be arriving at any moment. Suddenly I knew I had to do something major to get Derek out of the room.

A stunning plan suddenly **PINGED** into my head.

'Pete's got a brilliant model of a bus,' I told Uncle Boring.

Pete looked very puzzled, as well he might. 'Do I?' he asked.

'Yes, it's that old vintage one. I remember your mum put it up in your loft.'

'She did?' Pete still looked puzzled. I made frantic signs at him that we should get Uncle Boring up into the attic.

'I'd be very interested to see that,' droned Uncle Boring. Hooray! I actually began to like him for a second or two.

'You could go up and look at it,' I suggested. 'Pete, show your uncle where the hatch is and the stepladder.' And I silently mouthed 'DO IT!' at the same time.

WHAT'S GOING ON?

At last Pete moved. 'Come on,' he said and we all trooped upstairs.

90

I wouldn't
trust either
of them.

'We have to get him out of the room downstairs,' I whispered.

'Why?'

'Trust me,' I answered. Well, that put him on instant alert!

'Casper, what are you up to?'

'Look, there's the hatch!' I cried. 'And there's the stepladder. Up you go. I think the bus is at the back somewhere.'

Uncle Boring rubbed his hands together. 'Right-ho. This is very exciting. A vintage model bus. Wonderful. Up I go. Switch on the light. It's at the back somewhere, you say. Right-ho.'

And Uncle Boring disappeared into the loft, burbling to himself. I quietly closed the hatch and removed the stepladder.

Pete gripped my arm. 'What are you doing?' he demanded.

DING DONG!

Saved by the doorbell! Mr Butternut at last!

'Come on,' I said brightly. 'You've got visitors.'

I raced downstairs, opened the door and there was – MY MUM!

Mum looked very surprised. (No wonder!)

'Really?' She looked at her feet and shook her

head. 'No. They're fine.'

'Never mind,' laughed Mrs Jawolski. 'Come and help me in the kitchen.'

Pete grabbed my arm again and dragged me away from them. 'Will you tell me what's going on?'

Saved again. That doorbell was doing a grand job! Surely it had to be Mr Butternut this time. Now everything would be all right, wouldn't it?

NO, IT WOULDN'T!!

MY MUM came hurrying through from the kitchen.

SHE WAS ONLY GOING TO ANSWER THE DOOR!

NOOOOooo!

Pete's mum was supposed to answer the door, not mine! Now Mr Butternut was standing on the doorstep, smiling at MY MUM!

'Goodness me,' said Mr Butternut, 'I didn't realize you were so young.'

My mum blushed. SHE BLUSHED! IT WASN'T SUPPOSED TO BE LIKE THIS! Mr B was supposed to fall in love with Pete's mum, not mine!

At that moment Pete's mum appeared from the kitchen. 'Who is it?' she asked.

My teacher smiled. 'Hello, everyone. I'm Mr Butternut from the school!'

Mr Butternut gave Pete a big wink. 'Peter left his sweatshirt in the classroom and as I was passing I thought I would just drop it in.' And he winked at Pete again.

'That's very kind of you,' smiled Pete's mum. Good, this was getting better. 'Would you like to come in for some tea?'

Brilliant! Hooray! It was working!

'That's kind of you,' said Mr Butternut, 'but my wife and baby are waiting in the car. We're just off to get the weekend shopping.'

WIFE AND BABY!

MR BUTTERNUT WASN'T SUPPOSED
TO HAVE A WIFE AND BABY!

WHAT DID HE HAVE TO GO AND DO
THAT FOR?

And so Mr Butternut left – with his wife and
baby. Huh.

Pete's mum gazed around. 'Where's Derek?'
she asked. 'He was here a moment ago.'

I THINK CASPER MIGHT KNOW.

UM, HE'S LOOKING FOR SOMETHING.

I hoped nobody else could hear the distant thumps coming from somewhere up above. Not to mention the odd cry.

And then we had tea.

And after tea my mum went home.

And then Pete started.

'YOU INVITED BUTTERNUT TO TEA, DIDN'T YOU? I BET YOU WROTE SOME STUPID, CRUMBY LETTER! HE KEPT WINKING AT ME! YOU'VE MADE ME LOOK LIKE A COMPLETE IDIOT. YOU ARE MR STUPIDO AND I HATE YOU!'

Pete hurled himself at me. There was only one thing to do. It was time for some superheroics.

WHAM-BAM-
Jelly-AND-Jam!

PLEASE TURN
OVER!

101

I'm so glad I'm a chameleon.

So we made up and were friends again and we all lived happily ever after. In fact we ended up thinking it was pretty funny. I wonder if Uncle Boring has found that non-existent toy bus yet?

HELP! LET ME OUT!

That's the noise Mr Butternut makes when he's got a cold. It's like a mega-major explosion, I can tell you. The classroom walls shake! The windows fall out! The roof takes off!

That teacher of ours can certainly sneeze. If there was a sneezing competition in the Olympic Games, I bet Mr Butternut would win by miles. You could use Mr Butternut's sneezes to send a rocket into space.

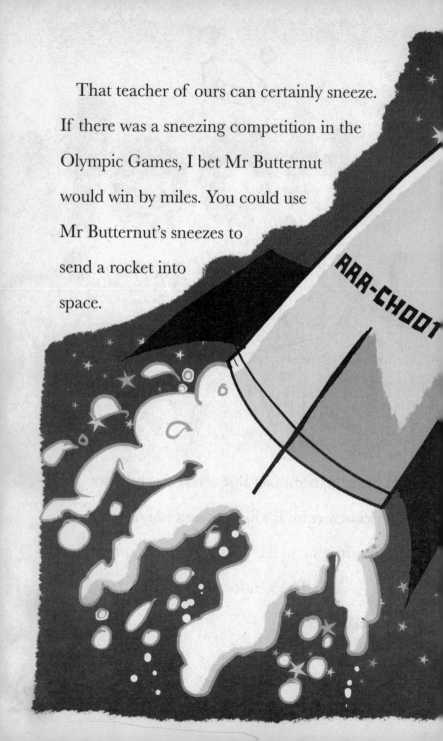

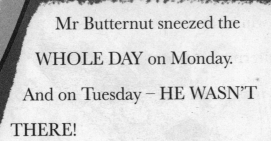

Mr Butternut sneezed the
WHOLE DAY on Monday.
And on Tuesday – HE WASN'T
THERE!

'He's probably blown himself up,'
Pete said.

'He shouldn't sneeze like that,'
muttered Noella Niblet, who is the
biggest sulkpot in history. 'He'll spread
germs everywhere. He's probably given
us all colds.'

Tyson's eyes boggled. 'We could all die!' he whispered in alarm. But then Tyson is scared of everything – even his own shoelaces.

Hartley Tartly-Green pushed his nose into the air. 'My mum says, "Sneeze on Monday and it will snow. Sneeze on Tuesday – the snow will go. Sneeze on Wednesday, it will be fine; sneeze on Thursday and the sun will shine. Sneeze on Friday – it'll be windy; sneeze on Sat–"'

'STOP!' yelled Pete. 'Sneezing has nothing to do with the weather. If you sneeze all that much – you know what? YOU'VE GOT A COLD, MR STUPIDO!'

'Well, my mum –' began Hartley.

'– is *Mrs* Stupido,' Pete slapped in.

Hartley sniffed and shut up. Hooray.

We were standing on the classroom steps, waiting for Miss Scratchitt, our headteacher, to come and open up, but she didn't. Instead, after a while, we saw a large figure approaching – a VERY large figure. It looked like a gigantic, swollen potato with a tiny head

perched on top. It was definitely heading our way.

'That's not Miss Scratchitt,' said Hartley Tartly-Green, as if we couldn't see that for ourselves.

'You should be a detective, Hartley,' murmured Sarah Sitterbout. He smiled back at her proudly and nodded.

By this time we could see that the figure wasn't a gigantic potato after all. It was a woman as big as Mount Everest.

The mountain heaved itself up the steps, shoved a key in the classroom door and flung it open.

'Inside!' she boomed.

She stomped in after us, threw her bulging bag down to the floor and overflowed into Mr Butternut's chair. She opened her bag, put a pile of chocolate bars on the desk, stripped the foil off two and shoved them into her mouth.

She glared at us, one by one. I swear I could see little red dots pinging out of her eyes and striking us. We sat there, frozen with fear, like scared rabbits.

'My name,' the mountain declared, 'is Mrs Cloddle. Mr Butternut is ill. He won't be back. I'm in charge now. Mrs Cloddle.'

Phew! Pete kicked me under the table. We exchanged pained looks with each other. A living nightmare had just taken over our class!

'You boys!' Mrs Cloddle roared. 'What are you pulling those stupid faces for!'

Pete and I had both turned round to see who she was talking to before we realized,

WITH BLOOD-CHILLING HORROR

that she was speaking to US!

'Yes – you two! Stand up when I talk to you! Pulling stupid faces – what was that about?'

'Nothing,' I murmured.

'Nothing? Do you mean you pull silly faces for no reason at all?'

Mrs Cloddle's eyes narrowed to tiny slits.

The red dots came streaming out like tiny

machine-gun bullets. She was melting my brain.

'I said NO ARGUING,' she spluttered, spraying bits of chocolate in all directions. Poor Noella Niblet and Hartley Tartly on the front table got splattered.

Mrs Cloddle gunned me and Pete with her dotty eyes. 'You two will stay behind at playtime and write out one hundred times: *I must not argue with Mrs Cloddle because she is always right.* Understood?'

GULP! We sat down. That Mrs Cloddle was a MONSTER. In fact all the time I'd been watching her I'd been drawing and when I looked down, guess what I'd drawn?

CLODZILLA!

I passed it to Pete. He gave a loud snort of laughter, clapped a hand to his mouth and hastily looked up to see if Mrs Cloddle had noticed. She had.

'You again!' roared Mrs Cloddle. 'Bring that piece of paper here.'

Pete took my drawing, pushed back his chair and walked up to Mrs Cloddle's desk. She stretched out a fat, sweaty, choccy-fingered hand.

'Give it to me.'

Pete lifted his hand, my drawing grasped firmly between his fingers and thumb. His hand went towards Mrs Cloddle's. She reached out for it and –

SWOOOOSH!

For a few seconds Mrs Cloddle was gobsmacked. Her eyes boggled. Her mouth fell open. (She looked a bit like a frog!) Meanwhile Pete chewed and chewed on the drawing and finally swallowed it. He had turned very white. (That was because of Mrs Cloddle, not because he'd eaten my picture.)

A smile came to Mrs Cloddle's face. It was like the smile you get from a crocodile before they bite your legs off.

'I suppose you think that's clever,' Mrs Cloddle snarled. 'Don't think I don't know what was on that paper, because I do.'

OH YES? DURRRR! WE'RE NOT STUPID, MRS CLODDLE! YOU COULDN'T POSSIBLY KNOW!

Everyone in class knew Mrs Cloddle didn't know, even Hartley Tartly-Green. Mrs Cloddle went on.

'Well, you are not the least bit clever. Not only do I know what was on that paper, but I am going to tell the head teacher. And after school I am going to tell your parents and everyone in your house, EVEN YOUR PET!

I don't care. I'm a chameleon, not a head teacher.

Also, you will miss lunch because you've just had something to eat and certainly don't need anything more.'

Mrs Cloddle's blazing eyes swept over Pete. She grabbed two more chocolate bars, stuffed them in her mouth and sniffed.

Pete came back and slumped into his seat.

I patted his back comfortingly.

'Sorry,' I whispered.

'Good picture,' he murmured back. 'It tasted lovely.'

YUM!

The rest of the morning passed in a long, boring silence. Mrs Cloddle was the complete opposite of Mr Butternut. He was funny and cheerful and made us laugh. He talked about anything and everything. He showed us things and told us stories. He made us feel good. We even got to like his beard. AND he told us we were all superheroes. But that Mrs Cloddle was like an iceberg.

When lunchtime came we had to leave Pete stuck in the classroom all on his own.

'I can see this class from the staffroom,' warned Mrs Cloddle.

'So don't think you can sneak out!'

Mia and I managed to beg a few unwanted sandwiches from some of our mates, and some lettuce and tomatoes. I stuffed them in

my pocket. I reckoned that Mrs Cloddle couldn't see *into* the class from the staffroom.

And she certainly couldn't see the *other side* of the class.

I went right round the back of the school until finally I reached our classroom, where Mrs Cloddle couldn't see me. I tapped on the window and Pete came scurrying over.

'Here's some food for you.'

Anyway, we somehow managed to get through the afternoon and then we were allowed to go home.

'We've got to get Mr Butternut back before we get killed by Clodzilla,' I told Pete.

'Horrible Hairy Face is ill,' Pete said gloomily.

'Then we'll have to make sure he gets better very quickly. I'm going to look up cures for colds on the computer when I get home.'

Of course, when I got in, big sis Abbie was already hogging the computer.

I BET YOU'RE LOOKING FOR A NEW BOYFRIEND.

'No, I'm not!' she squawked far too loudly, which meant she definitely was. 'I've already got a boyfriend, so there, and don't ask who he is because I shan't tell.'

'That's because he doesn't have a name because he DOESN'T EXIST,' I said. 'Anyhow, I have homework to do and I need the computer.'

'Tough,' said Abbie.

See? That's what my big sis is like. She's a big pain in the you-know-what.

Luckily Abbie got a call on her mobile from one of her friends and she was off and away, whispering and sniggering for HOURS. You know how it is.

I got down to it on the computer and was busy making lots of notes when Pete turned up. As usual.

'It says here that a hot bath can help cure a cold,' I told him.

'Great. Let's go to Mr Butternut's house and give him a hot bath,' Pete said stonily.

I didn't think Pete was being very helpful. I showed him the list I'd made so far.

AAAA-CHOO!

HOW TO HELP GET RID OF A COLD

★ a deep, hot bath - the steam helps

and the bath relaxes the body

Yuck!

★ hot soup - chicken noodle soup is good

★ vitamin C from oranges, lemons, etc.

★ have a sauna   HOT?

★ eat garlic and cauliflower

★ lemon and honey are good.

MMMM!

HONEY

'See?' I said. 'There are loads of things you can do to get better. Pass the phone.'

I dialled directory enquiries, got connected and a woman answered. It must have been his wife. I put on my deepest, growliest voice.

I slammed down the phone. Pete gave me an icy stare.

'That went well, Doctor Deathbreath. And I'm Doctor Doctor, am I? That was very imaginative of you.'

'Look,' I said. 'We had to do something. At least I tried. We are not going to survive Clodzilla more than another day.'

'Hmmm,' Pete grunted. 'Maybe we should all have colds tomorrow and stay off school.'

But of course the next day there wasn't a sneeze between us. At school Pete and I found the others waiting for us on the classroom steps. You've never seen such a miserable lot, and school hadn't even started.

'Mithter Butternut is still off thick,'
Lucy declared. 'I thaw Mithuth Cloddle
arrive thith morning.'

Lucy always speaks like that. She's got
the biggest teeth brace in history and it
makes her lisp. (We call her The Mighty
Munch!) But you should see her in gym.
She can climb ropes faster than Tarzan
and she's brilliant at cartwheels. The
last time I tried a cartwheel I almost
knocked out Mr Butternut. He was
trying to help me and my foot caught

him right on the chin.

'What are we going to do?' asked Sarah. 'I don't think I can survive another day with Clodzilla.'

But nobody could think of ANYTHING. Mrs Cloddle came heaving across the playground with her bag of choccy bars while we were still hammering away at our brains.

'Inside,' Mrs Cloddle ordered and we all trooped in. Another miserable day was about to begin.

AND THEN IT HAPPENED . . .

CLODZILLA SNEEZED.

For two seconds Mrs Cloddle looked totally
startled, as if a bomb had gone off up her
nose. (Which it had, sort of.) Then she gave a
ginormous sniff and wiped her nose with her
sleeve.

That Mrs Cloddle was more disgusting than
a squashed slug. (Which is what her sleeve now
looked like.)

Hartley Tartly-Green was waving his arm in
the air.

'What?' snapped Mrs Cloddle.

'My mum says, "Sneeze on Monday and it will snow. Sneeze on Tuesday – the snow will go. Sneeze on Wednesday, it will be fine; sneeze on Thurs–'

'ENOUGH!' roared Mrs Cloddle.

Poor Hartley. You could almost see his heart sticking to the ceiling where it had leaped out of his body.

Pete nudged me and stuck his arm up.

'What now?' sniffed Mrs Cloddle.

'My dad says that if you pinch your nose when you sneeze, your eyeballs **SPING** out of their sockets and just dangle from your face.'

I grinned and shoved my hand in the air. 'And my aunt says that when you sneeze, a billion germs come shooting out of your nostrils at a gazillion trillion miles an hour.'

Mrs Cloddle was just opening her mouth to speak when Mia waved her arm.

'My granny says that if you keep a large lettuce leaf stuck up each nostril, it stops you from sneezing at all.'

'And if you stick your head underwater,' Pete added, 'you definitely won't sneeze EVER.'

It seemed as if Mrs Cloddle had swollen to twice her normal size. And considering she had started as big as Mount Everest, she was now

EEEE-NORMOUS!

'You will all stay in at lunchtime and not have ANY lunch,' she bellowed. 'And you will ALL write out FIFTY BILLION TIMES – *I must not talk twaddle in class.* IS THAT UNDERSTOOD?'

Mrs Cloddle glared at us, daring any one of us to argue.

Well! How unfair was that? We were too shocked to argue. How dare she keep us in at lunchtime? How dare she make us miss our lunch? There was only one thing to do. It was time for –

WHAM-BAM-Jelly-AND-Jam!

PLEASE TURN OVER!

147

In fact, just as Mrs Cloddle finished telling us
we had fifty billion lines to write out, the door
opened and guess who walked in?

MR HORRIBLE HAIRY FACE!

Except that he didn't look horrible to us at
all. He looked like a REAL SUPERHERO!

Mrs Cloddle seethed like a snake in a sack.

'You are welcome to your class. I have never met such awful children.'

Mr Butternut looked shocked and surprised. He gazed at every one of us, searching our faces. Then he turned to Mrs Cloddle.

'I think you are mistaken,' he said. 'It's the other way round. They have never met such an awful teacher. Please leave immediately.'

Mrs Cloddle's jaw just about fell off her face. She turned a deep red, which then changed to white anger. She packed her bag furiously and steamed out of the classroom, knocking things flying as she went. She slammed the door behind her. She had hardly taken two steps outside when we heard the

most gigantic explosion.

ACHOOOO!

Even the windows rattled. Poor Clodzilla!

Mr Butternut went to his desk and sat down.

We grinned back at him.

WELL THEN,
WE ARE BACK TOGETHER
AGAIN. I BELIEVE YOU HAVE
FIFTY BILLION LINES
TO WRITE . . .

Fifty
billion lines?
Easy-peasy!

It all started with a Scarecrow.

Puffin is seventy years old.
Sounds ancient, doesn't it? But Puffin has never been
so lively. We're always on the lookout for the next big
idea, which is how it began all those years ago.

Penguin Books was a big idea from the mind of
a man called Allen Lane, who in 1935 invented
the quality paperback and changed the world.
**And from great Penguins, great Puffins grew,
changing the face of children's books forever.**

The first four Puffin Picture Books were hatched in 1940 and the
first Puffin story book featured a man with broomstick arms called
Worzel Gummidge. In 1967 Kaye Webb, Puffin Editor, started the
Puffin Club, promising to **'make children into readers'**.
She kept that promise and over 200,000 children became
devoted Puffineers through their quarterly instalments of
Puffin Post, which is now back for a new generation.

Many years from now, we hope you'll look back and
remember Puffin with a smile. **No matter what your age
or what you're into, there's a Puffin for everyone.**
The possibilities are endless, but one thing is for sure:
whether it's a picture book or a paperback, a sticker book
or a hardback, **if it's got that little Puffin
on it – it's bound to be good.**